THE LAST ADVENTURE AS NAMELESS

R.B.M.PATEL

EDITED BY ANGELICA WILSON
ILLUSTRATIONS BY JADE MARIE MACMILLAN

authorHOUSE

AuthorHouse™
1663 Liberty Drive
Bloomington, IN 47403
www.authorhouse.com
Phone: 833-262-8899

© 2023 R.B.M.Patel. All rights reserved.

No part of this book may be reproduced, stored in a retrieval system, or transmitted by any means without the written permission of the author.

This is a work of fiction. All of the characters, names, incidents, organizations, and dialogue in this novel are either the products of the author's imagination or are used fictitiously.

Published by AuthorHouse 04/21/2023

ISBN: 979-8-8230-0166-3 (sc)
ISBN: 979-8-8230-0164-9 (hc)
ISBN: 979-8-8230-0165-6 (e)

Library of Congress Control Number: 2023903355

Print information available on the last page.

Any people depicted in stock imagery provided by Getty Images are models, and such images are being used for illustrative purposes only. Certain stock imagery © Getty Images.

This book is printed on acid-free paper.

Because of the dynamic nature of the Internet, any web addresses or links contained in this book may have changed since publication and may no longer be valid. The views expressed in this work are solely those of the author and do not necessarily reflect the views of the publisher, and the publisher hereby disclaims any responsibility for them.

CONTENTS

The Great Fall 1
The Great Sleeps 5
Heyhin Berum; Land Of The Longtail 13
Kartik & Tejuin 35
Goodboy 47

For my niece, sister's sons and their cousin

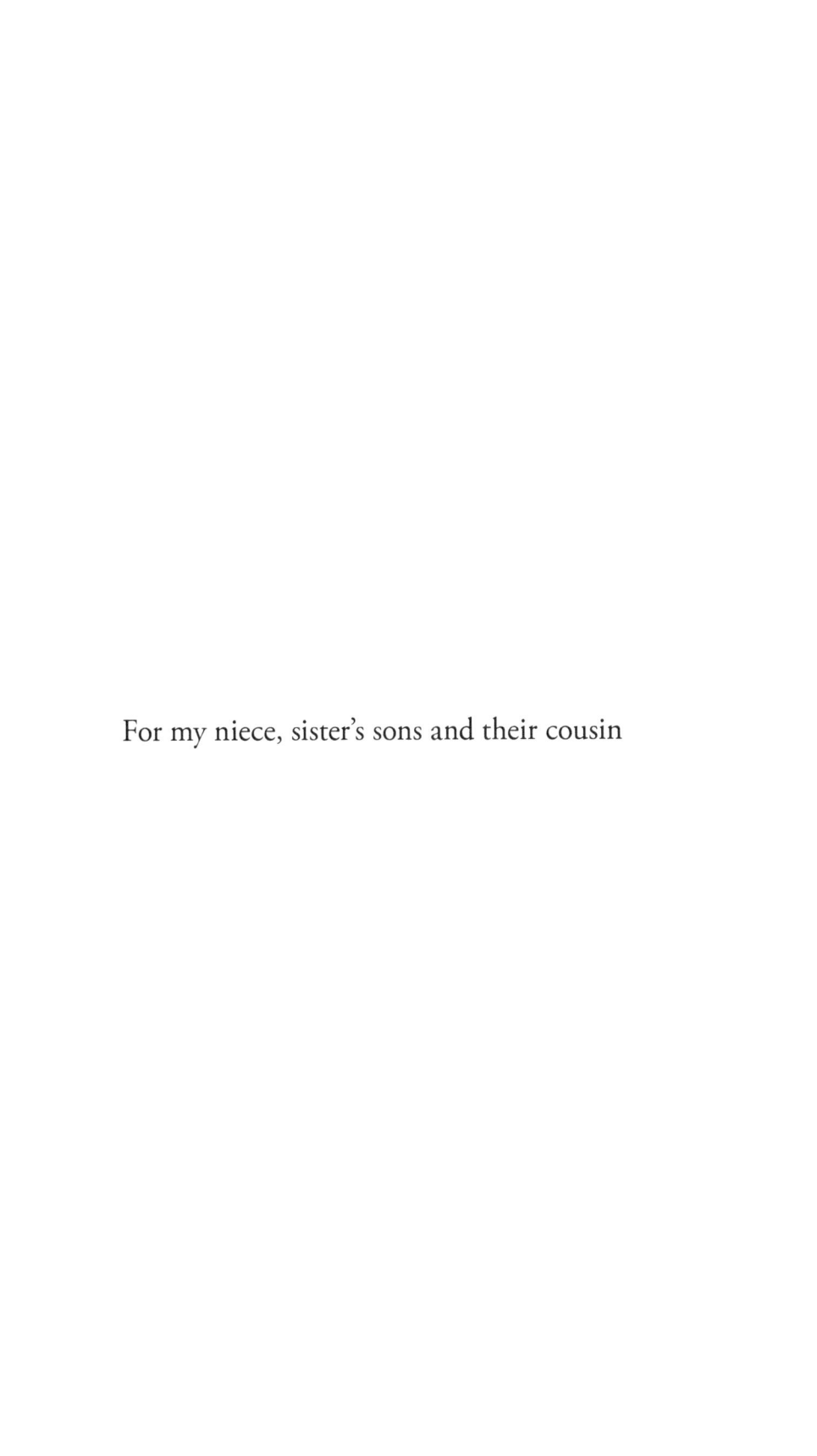

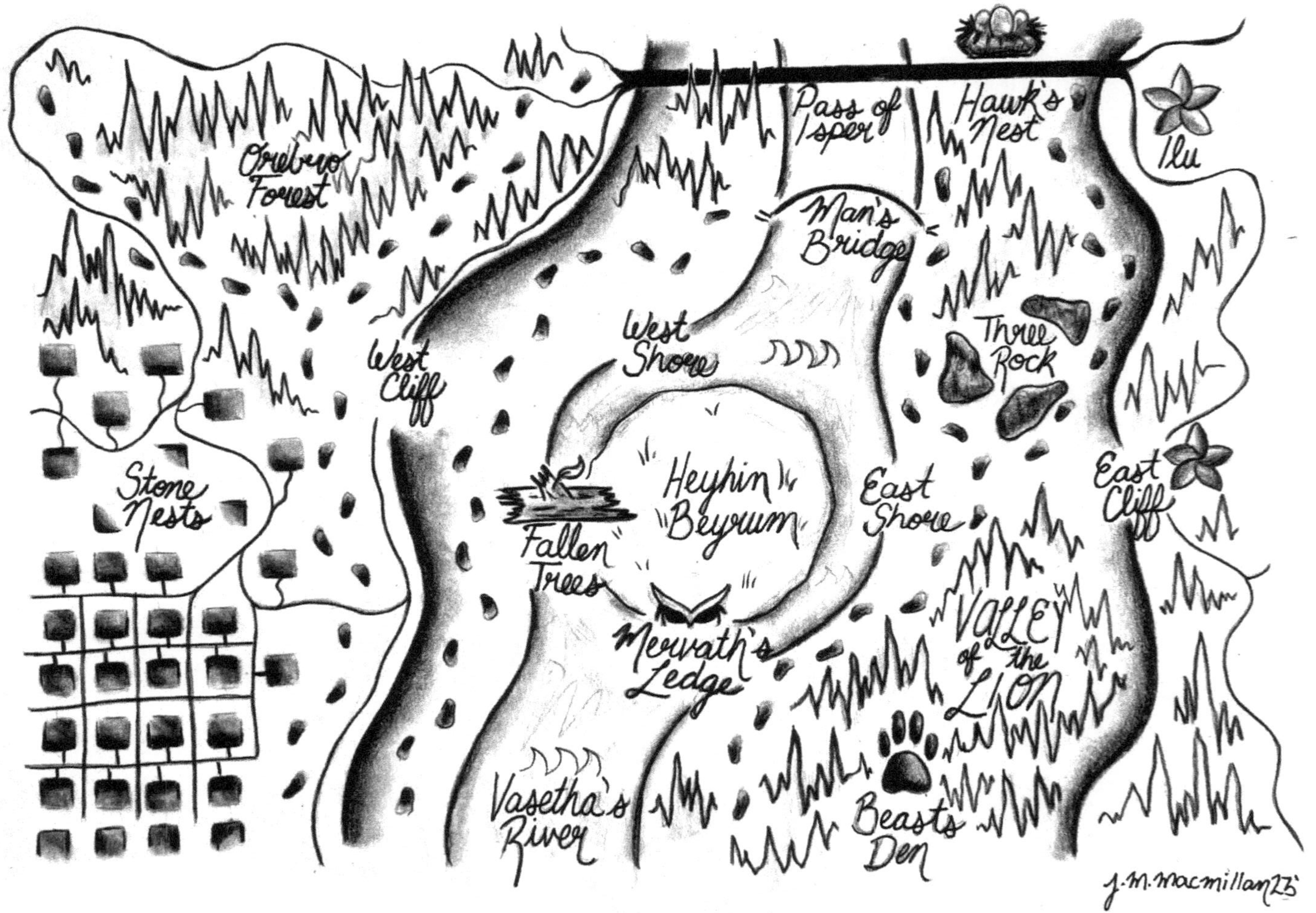

Orebro Forest
Pass of Isper
Hawk's Nest
Ilu
Man's Bridge
West Shore
Three Rock
West Cliff
Heyhin Beyrum
East Shore
East Cliff
Stone Nests
Fallen Trees
Merwath's Ledge
Valley of the Lion
Vasetha's River
Beasts Den
J.M. Macmillan 23

THE GREAT FALL

I recall the first cold, like a wound to the heart. Eyes I did have but could not see, for they were not ready for the world. The chill was all around but I was not alone, there were others like me, cold and in the dark. Together we tried best we could to share our warmth. We were new but learned fast that we needed each other. Safe we thought we were, yet not from the wind and cold. Come often did the Great Warmth from before the cold. She was soft and rested with us, never long enough. The Great Warmth kept us clean as we moved, she was burdened with our protection. Movement away from the others was not safe so the Great Warmth tried to keep us together. Often when she left we hungered and reached out into the cold darkness, learning what we could of the nest. The cold was too much to be independent, we always returned to the others quickly. We waited for the Great Warmth to return, and with her warmth came the rest we needed. I am tired from being without the Great Warmth, she is all I need.

Again I awoke to the cries of my brethren and no warmth. Many sleeps have passed and we grow stronger, but still so cold. The wind blew louder than ever before and I reached out for the Great Warmth but she was beyond my grasp. One moment without the Great Warmth felt like a lifetime, nothing else mattered except her warmth. I hear the others cry and I feel their pain, for a life without warmth is a life I cannot bare. Still there is no sight but The Glow we all see. If you pay heed, the Great Warmth is away often when The Glow is strong. The Glow brings warmth, not as that of the Great, but enough to notice and enough to test the limits of bravery when the Great Warmth is away. Can it be that I can find the Great Warmth while The Glow is strong? For I need her. That need fueled the first turn. That need was the last time I was with the others, and the first time I knew pain not of my physical form.

As it happens it wasn't a turn, but a fall, and I was alone without the Great Warmth or the others that the Great

Warmth cared for. I do not know how far I fell but it hurt, and the cold was stronger. I had no one else to keep me warm and I cried, louder than I ever cried before as I came to realize I had lost the company of my brothers and sisters. I wanted to rest but it was too cold, so I cried and waited for the Great Warmth but she did not come. Soon The Glow receded from my shut eyes and the cold wind grew ever stronger. I had no choice but to look for warmth. I was alone and scared, new sounds near and far, some so loud it raised the greatest fears I had but did not yet understand. I could hear my brothers and sisters cries but they were beyond reach, and things beyond my reach at that time might as well not be there.

I cried what I thought was my last cry. I was lost, alone, hungry, scared and colder than I can remember without the Great Warmth. When it seemed all hope was lost I was scooped up and taken away from the cold. It wasn't the Great Warmth but it mattered not for I was comfortable and safe. The day of the fall and cold was over. Voices I heard and breathing like no other, loud like the wind. I didn't have the strength left for fear so I slept in the new warm, where there was no wind and I dreamed of the Great Warmth.

THE GREAT SLEEPS

Many moons had passed since the Great Fall but of late I did not dwell on that, for days and nights were warm and food was plentiful. Strange though it was; milk from a tube and not the Great Warmth. My protector whispered to me, for he worried about my well being as I was so small. Do not laugh at the name for I carried it with pride for a time, but he called me The Baby, and the beast was named Goodboy. When he spoke to me it was always to reassure me that I was safe in his home and that I could sleep without worry. So I did, and I grew stronger. Then the unexpected occurred without warning, The Glow turned into The Light and I could see! All was obscured like the fog of a spring morning. When the fog lifted I gazed upon my protector for the first time. Hairless and smooth like my hands but all over, and of a size I could not comprehend at the time for even though I had grown I was small in his hands. He was of the race of men and tall he was, so Tall is how I thought of him. Then I heard the breathing of the beast and was confronted by a giant nose and eyes as big as my head! Breath like a dragon and teeth of a lion! But in his eyes I saw not that of any malice, but the eyes of friendship. Still, at first I was scared, for all was new and Goodboy was large, not like the Tall but with four legs, fast and strong. And so it was that Goodboy would also be my protector in my days of youth. He would watch as I slept and grew. He loved me as a brother always and as time passed I learned to love him back.

The first time I saw the sun I understood The Glow from before I could see, for the sun is the strongest of all things beyond all realms and is so far beyond the skies we see that it does not burn but warms us, the first Great Warmth and giver to all who need the warm. My Tall and Goodboy always stood watch as I played and learned of the world. My Tall rejoiced at my growth and strength, and Goodboy jumped and laughed, his roar shook the earth as a warning to all but I did not feel fear, for he was my Goodboy.

Days of play and snacks quickly turned to training. Climbing was hard but made my limbs stronger, and learning to find food and store it was essential. I was happy in those days to be with my Tall and Goodboy in the stone lands of men but my Tall was sad at times when he spoke to me. He told me that in these days I would be safe and warm but soon, before I was ready, I would have to travel and find my own way, for the land of the Tall and beasts is not my home, and he would not give me a name but like him I would find my name, when I find my strength it would come. I cared not for I was The Baby and my focus was on learning all that is new of the world. Learning of trees I loved, so many kinds in all shapes and textures, and natural was my ability to climb and jump. I grew in these days, my fur began to thicken and from within my own warmth grew. The feasts were plentiful, with more variety then I would see in my time but I did not overindulge, for my Tall frequently reminded me that food would not always be easy to obtain and we must store for the winter to come, when the trees sleep and bare not fruit or nut. Hard lessons for someone so small. So I listened to what I could in the hopes it would avail me in the years to come.

It will not be forgotten, the deeds of my Tall, even though he warns of his own kind and of beasts that are not Goodboy, the world I am to set forth unto seems more and more harsh. My Tall tells me of the flying beasts; some are small and sing songs of Florian, others have claws and sharp teeth. They may be my greatest threat, for they glide silent and see all that moves from high above the tallest trees. My Tall warns that I must be wary of all others not of my kind but to not walk in fear of others, for the great sun has provided unmatched speed and agility for which my kind will use to flourish.

We traveled what I thought was far, my Tall and Goodboy showed me much of their lands, the stone nests, fields clear and wide in which the sun lay no shadow. Often we did look for trees under which we would shelter from the sun, for the sun gives much but we must not over feast in its glory because although the fires burn far they can still burn slowly in the heat of the summer. When I thought it would be impossible to survive the heat the rains came and with them the sun and warmth hid while we cooled, the rivers swelled and much washed away. Again came warnings from my Tall; one raindrop can quench your thirst but the river can wash away all that you care for, safety in the high ground was the way of my kind but trees are not always safe either, for the Tall cut them down so they can build and they do not stop. When the rains ceased the green of all flourished, wondrous colors and smells and the world was alive under the sun. We saw many Tall and many four legged beasts of all sizes and shapes. Not all four legged beasts are friendly, for my kind and the beasts dispute territories of the Tall. Paths and trees that belong to us are guarded from all by the beasts. Others of my kind I did see briefly but in their eyes was only fear for Goodboy. In the realm of Goodboy I was safe to go as I pleased but no others of my kind were safe, for I was his baby and he guarded me always.

My Tall grew sad under his smile as summer passed, although we played he did not rejoice with Goodboy and I. He spoke of the time that approaches, the time I would have to find my way to my kind. I thought often of the Great Warmth that I began with and if I could find her. Could I find my brothers and sisters? Would I know them? Would they know me? Where would I look? Closed were my eyes during the Great Fall but to dwell on that would drive me to sadness so I must focus on what I have learned from my Tall and prepare best I can for the hard times to come, as foretold by my Tall. The day came and we ventured further than ever before, beyond the fields and stone nests of the Tall. Down we went to the river, loud and furious it was and surrounded by my trees, taller than the trees I'd seen in the past, old as the dirt and thick as a Tall. There were many of my kind of all sorts of browns, grays, blacks, and mixed markings. For the first time I looked closer at myself, mostly black with some gray, and some brown. More so I wondered what my Great Warmth or brothers and sisters looked like. There were song birds which usually made my Tall happy, but not this day, this day was our last. We sat many hours by the Three Rock and over the small bridge that connected the valley. My Tall was sad but also happy, I can't understand how hard it must be for him to let his baby go. It did not take long for me to climb and jump from giant tree to giant tree, more trees than I've ever seen, and so many of my kind, so busy that I seemed to go unnoticed. Time passed and I played and chased and was chased in the funnest games ever. I had forgotten about my Tall and Goodboy for they could not climb and follow to play with me. When I climbed back down they were gone, that was the second time I lost the warmth I loved and even though I had warning, it hurt no less. I will remember my

Tall and all he did for me after the Great Fall. Though I long to see him and Goodboy again I do not hold hope for it, but am glad for time spent in the safety of my Tall and the Great Sleeps I had to help me learn and grow.

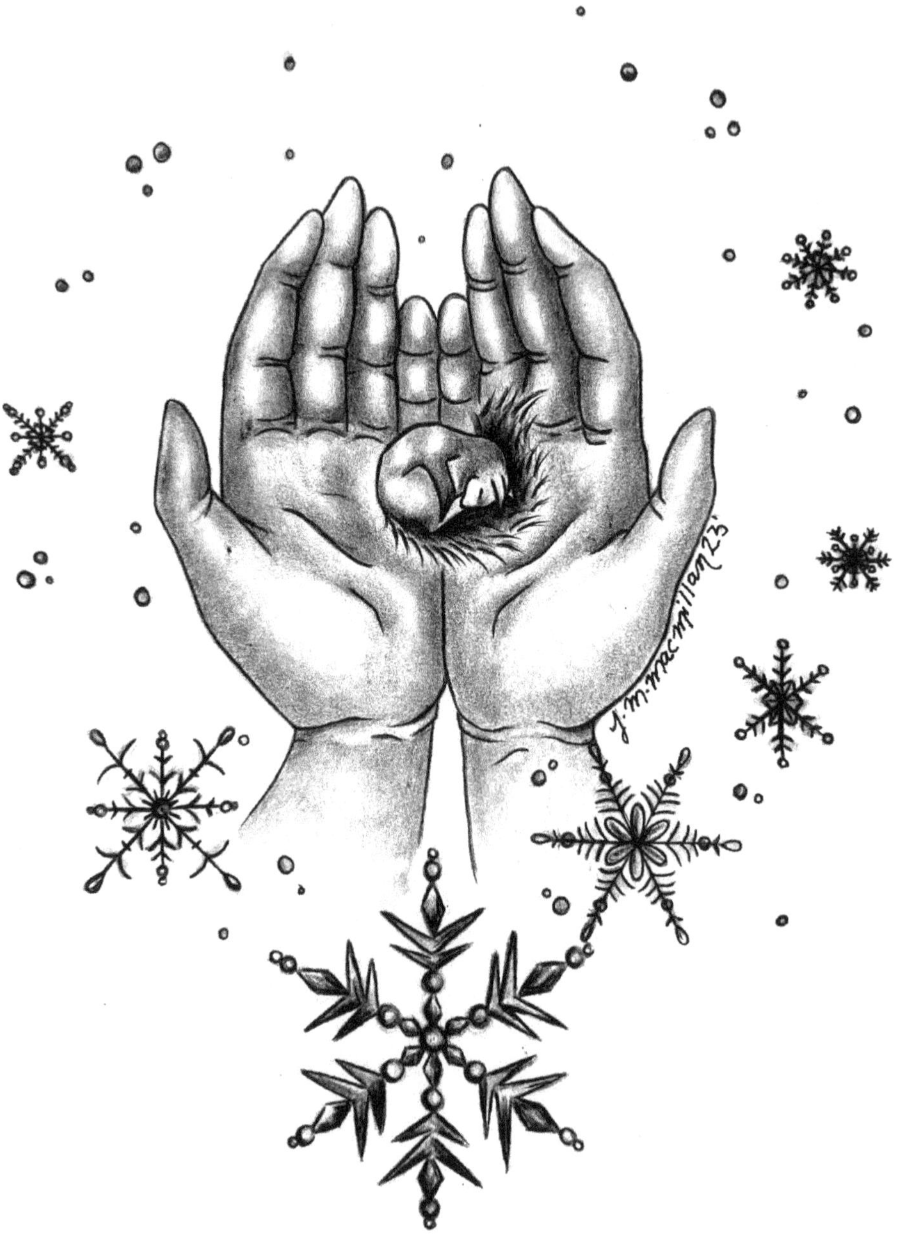
J.M.MacMillan23

HEYHIN BERUM;
LAND OF THE LONGTAIL

(hey-hin bey-rum)*

There I was alone, but not afraid, when I heard a voice. 'Estel, Estel! Come we are being called, Este - wait you're not Estel.'

Our eyes met.

'I don't know you, are you a visitor from beyond the valley? Where are you from? Why are you so clean? It has not rained. What is your name? I'm Chire and I'm looking for my brother, Estel.'

She spoke fast and I felt I needed to respond.

'I'm the bab...' but I did not finish. 'I'm not from here, I come from far, I was raised by the Tall and was released to find my way amongst my own, but I fear I am already lost.'

'The Tall!! They come here to enjoy the Valley Of The Lion, but they bring beasts with them, some bring food but the Elders are wary of the Tall. You didn't answer my question, what is your name?'

'I'm Nameless, for now.'

'Nameless? That's a silly name! Well come Nameless help me find Estel, for the dark of night quickly approaches. You will have to stay with us for the cold of night but I warn you, do not speak of the Tall to my father, for he is on the council and they do not trust the Tall.'

So I followed Chire through the trees until we came upon a giant one with many nests.

'Here, Nameless, is Heyhin Beyrum, the city of the Longtail of the Valley Of The Lion. Wait here and I will ask my mother if I may welcome a guest for the night.'

So up she climbed as I waited, whispers I could hear, then;

'There you are Estel! Where are mother and father?'

'In the upper nests for the night.'

'Well then come and meet my new friend, Nameless.'

'That's a funny name.'

'Yeah I know, he's not from the valley.'

'Well bring him up, night draws near.'

Quickly she came down, brought me up and introduced me to her brother Estel who was full grown. There was a seriousness to him, as if his days of play were behind him. We did not speak much that night, Estel told me when the sun rises I would have to consult with the council and their father, Eberges. Fast to sleep Estel and Chire went but my mind was racing, it seemed so much was happening so fast and it was the first time I was in a nest with eyes that could see. There were many materials and the roof seemed solid, no wind entered the nest, it was truly made by one with experience. Eventually I could stay awake no longer so I curled up beside my new friends, closed my eyes and let the sleep take me.

I opened my eyes to an empty nest and Chire shaking me to wake. 'Wake Nameless, big day today, come, come, the sun shines strong in the early.'

The sun did seem to shine bright that day, I could see all the nests and busy others, and the river and the edges of the valley above the trees, it was beautiful. At that moment Chire looked at me impatiently, she was so lovely. Up we went almost to the top of the tallest trees where a great many platforms of sticks were spread among the branches. On the various platforms were many Longtail of all shapes and sizes, it was obvious which was the main platform, at the center where everyone looked on quietly. Chire brought me forward, Estel was standing behind where the others sat and behind him perched a sky beast, round with piercing eyes, watching. My heartbeat quickened but I realized no one else was distressed by the beast so I tried best to hide the fear inside. One of the seated stood and spoke.

'Greetings traveler! And welcome to Heyhin Berum, city of the Longtail. I am Eberges and I speak for the council on this day, may I ask what shall we call thee?'

'I am Nameless, for the Tall that raised me said I would find my name when I find my strength.'

So I had forgotten not to mention the Tall, but my Tall had always told me to speak the truth, even when it will do you ill. For lying to others is lying to one's self.

'Raised by the Tall!' Eberges coughed out 'Excuse me but this is shocking news, while we have heard of tales of some Longtail raised by the Tall you are the first to be among us during this age.'

So I explained best I could about my Tall and Goodboy and how I ended up here. All were silent as I spoke, and my eyes kept a focus on the sky beast. '..and that's when I met Chire and she kept me safe through the night.'

After a brief silence and whispers among the council, Eberges spoke.

'Much to think about have we, young Longtail, for we do not trust the Tall and their doings, always cutting and building they are, with a thirst that destroys many homes, not just those of the Longtail. But rejoice for you are safe with us in The Valley Of The Lion. My daughter Chire will teach you the ways of our kind, for it will be her second winter and she knows what you will need to learn to survive. Grudgingly, we accept another mouth to feed but I see hope for you that you will find your name and help our kind. Masai, my wife, will find a place for a newcomer to live for she is the greatest of our nest builders and teacher to all.'

Eberges turned and spoke softly with the sky beast, thus marking the end of the council meeting, and everyone scurried off except for Estel and Chire.

Estel was the first to approach me.

'That went well Nameless, I feared for we do not trust things from beyond our lands, which is the way of most of the creatures, but it is plain to see you are a Longtail, lost though you may be. I will tell you that you most likely come from the land of the Tall and their stone nests, for there are trees there between the lanes and Longtail make nests there. Your Tall, who was like your mother, brought you here to be safe and live a true life of the free Longtail in the great Valley Of The Lion.'

Estel spoke calm and true as if his words were only spoken with great thought.

'Is there really a lion?' I blurted out, for it was my first of many questions.

'No, silly.' Chire squeaked in. 'There may be a cat or two roaming through the valley, but no lion or large cat for many ages. The tall keep small cats as guards of their stone nests but it is rare to see them beyond their homes. Unlike the four legged beasts that the Tall bring to adventure on the paths of the Tall, they come often but mostly stay on the path and only when the sun is awake.' Chire's voice was soft but confident like her father, Eberges and brother, Estel. 'Now come Nameless, we will bother Estel no more til late. First we will venture to meet my mother, Masai, and she will show you of our great nests.'

I followed Chire from tree to tree, other Longtail looked at me with suspicious eyes, I smiled a small smile and tried to keep up with Chire. She was fast and moved elegantly with little effort from branch to branch while I was slow and cautious, for we were high above the ground and my reach and grasp were not as strong as Chire's. We came to a large nest, I was exhausted from the journey while Chire was waiting with her impatient grin shining my way.

'If I was a cruel friend I would name you Slowpoke.'

I tried not to be embarrassed but I was. In we went to the nest, it was bright, for it had a clear top and all the walls were made of the same tree barks all aligned with great precision and care. Masai did not greet us for she was busy examining what looked like scratches on the wall. As Chire and I approached they seemed to be more like countings, as if to keep track of the world gone by. After a moment of silence Masai spoke.

'Chire I have decided that this Nameless will stay in the lower levels with you and the others of maturity but not wisdom.' Masai's voice was soft and slow, not from lack of confidence but from an abundance of sadness as if she carried the pain and responsibility of all.

'Yes mother.' Chire responded as if she hadn't any other response to give. 'Come now Nameless, there is much to see of our lands, and much danger to learn of.'

We left Masai as quietly as we entered.

'Wait Chire! I have a question before anything else, who was the great sky beast that was at the council meeting that Eberges spoke to? It's as if I still feel its eyes piercing me.'

'Oh, that's just old Mervath, he's an owl but fear not for he does not eat Longtail. When he was young he was separated from his family during a great storm and found safety here in the valley. It is said he has been here since the trees were small, but I doubt that. However, he did know Isper, my fathers fathers father. He also keeps the seven sister hawks from hunting us in Heyhin Berum. Mervath is wise but he also speaks in circles and sleeps much during the day, he hunts at night and watches our land. I'm sure you will have a chance to meet him soon, for he will have questions for a Longtail raised by the Tall. Come now Nameless, first I will show you all the glory of Heyhin Berum.'

That day Chire and I traveled around Heyhin Berum, she showed me all the trees that bare seed, nut, fruit and flower, the trees that keep their leaves all year, and the trees that the Longtail hollow and store seed, nut and all that is precious in order for us to survive the winter. Turns out Heyhin Berum is really an island in the valley, directed by the river Vasetha. The western slope of the island was sandy and had many routes for the Longtail to pass to the West Shore of the valley but none that land beast would travel, except for during the coldest of winters when the western flow of Vasetha might freeze. We came to the southern edge of the island where there is a cliff that overlooks much of the valley to the south and across the river Vasetha on both shores. Chire told me it was known as Mervath's Ledge and that if I brought him a mushroom from the West Shore he would answer any question I could have. He was not there at the time and I had no mushroom, so until another time. Great was the day following Chire around as she taught me all one could hope to know, night drew near and we headed back to the nests. Estel was waiting when we returned.

'I hope your day was prosperous, Nameless.'

'Yes it was, Chire knows much of the land and of preparations for winter.' I responded.

'Good, the sun will sleep soon. You will stay in the lower nests as Masai requests, I will stay in the nest below where I can be aware of all that moves, so sleep now knowing that you are safe and I will see you when the sun wakes.'

That night I slept well without the stress of tomorrow, for I was too tired to dwell on what the future will hold. My hands were warm with Chire's and my heart was at ease, for I knew I was a Longtail and not alone.

The days to come brought much change; the trees changed in color and then shed their leaves, the nights grew longer and Chire told me how the sun needs to rest more for winter but would return stronger in spring. Much knowledge did Chire possess, for she was the daughter of an elder of the council and much was to be expected of her. I learned that her brother Estel would one day sit on the council for he was a descendant of Isper.

While Chire and I explored the West Shore of the valley I asked her about Isper as there were many tales of the bravery of Isper. It is said he feared no beast of land or sky and that he traveled far beyond the lands of the Valley Of The Lion. He spoke with all; beasts, friends and the Tall that would visit. It is even said the Tall would come to the Valley Of The Lion just to see and speak with Isper, they would bring him fruits and seeds from far lands beyond the mountains of the north and waters of the south that Vasetha leads to.

'Come Nameless, and look to the wall of the valley of the West Shore. Do you see the break in the tree line?' Chire asked.

'Yes, it rises up to the top of the valley.' I replied.

'That is the Trail Of Isper, it leads to the river of stone nests where the Tall travel with great speed in their moving nests made of metal. Great danger is there and you mustn't travel over the Stone River unless in dire need. The Stone River leads to The Pass Of Isper, do you see the pass? It connects the Stone River over the Valley Of The Lion and was built by the Tall many ages ago. There the seven hawk sisters nest; Yarutas, Yanus, Yanom, Yaseut, Yasendew, Yasruht and Yairf, each one more deadly than the last. It is known that none escape their grasp. They are our greatest threat, even though they do not enter Heyhin Berum thanks to Mervath, they hunt all other lands and see all that moves. Not only are they sisters but mothers as well, many young they have to feed so one must be careful and stay hidden in the trees. It is said that Isper, many ages ago, climbed the pass from west to east over the Man's Bridge, past the Hawks Nests where he brought back the flower of Ilu which only grows on the East Cliffs, just so he could say he did it. And so it is named The Pass Of Isper. I have never been so close as to see the flower and would never consider taking the Pass of Isper. In days of recent, the Tall have built a small bridge over Vasetha that leads to the East Shore and Three Rock.'

'I do love the valley, Chire, it is all that my Tall spoke of when I was small. There are many song birds and other creatures such as us but I must ask of the three black birds that seem to be always present, together they are not, but still move in unison as three points of a triangled leaf?'

'Those are the ravens, they also watch all but do not hunt Longtail. It is said they will circle the dead, even before death, but come now Nameless, it is time to learn of the dangers of the East Shore and the wild beasts.'

The snows began to fall in the days we explored the East Shore. It is where the beasts with no master live, the gray wolves who hunt at night and do not live with, listen to or follow the Tall. They follow a leader of their own and dwell in the caves to the south on the East Shore. Wolves do not hunt the Longtail of the valley for we are swift as the wind and climb faster than the wolves. They hunt the Long-Ear who cannot climb and are scavengers of the night. The Tall fear the wolves for they outnumber many, it is said when you see one's eyes two more look alone at you from the darkness. There is no escape in the open fields from their pursuit and though they do not hunt us they will gladly eat us or feed us to their young. The wolves stay on the East Shore most of the year and are not seen in the sun but as winter approaches they have a longer domain of the valley and will venture to the West Shore if Vasetha should freeze. The East Shore also has many paths of the Tall, for in summer months they will bask in the glory of the valley. Few Tall visit during the winter, for they to must stay warm and safe.

'Come Nameless, look, mushrooms! Just what we needed, grab what you can and we will head back to Heyhim Berum and see if Mervath is at his Ledge.'

I was excited, for I knew the question I wished to ask Mervath, though I feared for the answer.

So we trekked back to the West Shore and over the fallen trees to Heyin Berum, it was a busy day with the winter almost at hand. I followed Chire to Mervath's Ledge where he sat silent, alone upon a branch with his back to us, snow building atop his head, surely he had not moved during the day. Chire pushed me forward and I stumbled as I approached wide, hoping to see Mervath's face. His eyes were closed but then one opened.

'Greetings young Longtail, the one raised by the Tall if I am correct.'

'Greetings great Mervath, I am the one raised by the Tall, but how did you know?'

'I see and hear much Nameless, and you have a scent that is not of the valley. Come close, do not fear, for I am friend of all Longtail. I see you have brought me a mushroom, possibly the last of the year. I thank you and young Chire, daughter of Eberges, for I see she has guided you well since your arrival. I have many questions I wish to ask you young Nameless, of the Tall I have pondered much to which you might possess insight but first I know there is something you wish to ask, something that burns in you.'

'Yes Mervath, there is, though I would have many questions for you as well, one burns in me strongly. Will I find my Great Warmth that I know is my mother? Will I find my brothers and sisters? I know they do not dwell in these lands, so is it my destiny to go in search and find them?'

'Much you ask in one question, I will do what I can to answer. Many Longtails live in the trees by the lands of the Tall in their stone nests, and many of their young are lost, for there are many perils in the land of the Tall. Some lost young are found by their mothers, sadly some are not and perish, for young Longtails require much love and attention. Some Longtails like you are taken by the Tall and cared for before being released, few of these Longtail are in these lands. If you search for your mother in the land of the stone nests you might find her, you might not. She might not recognize you as you are, and if you were lost before sight how would you recognize her? She is beyond this land and my protection, if you travel to find her there is no guarantee of your return, for you may become lost in your journey. But now is not the time to worry, for you must survive your first winter. In spring we will speak of this quest and whether or not it is feasible. I am sorry that my answer is not the answer you were searching for but there is hope. During the winter you will come visit me and we will speak of many things. Now I must stretch my wings and you must return to the nests before dark.'

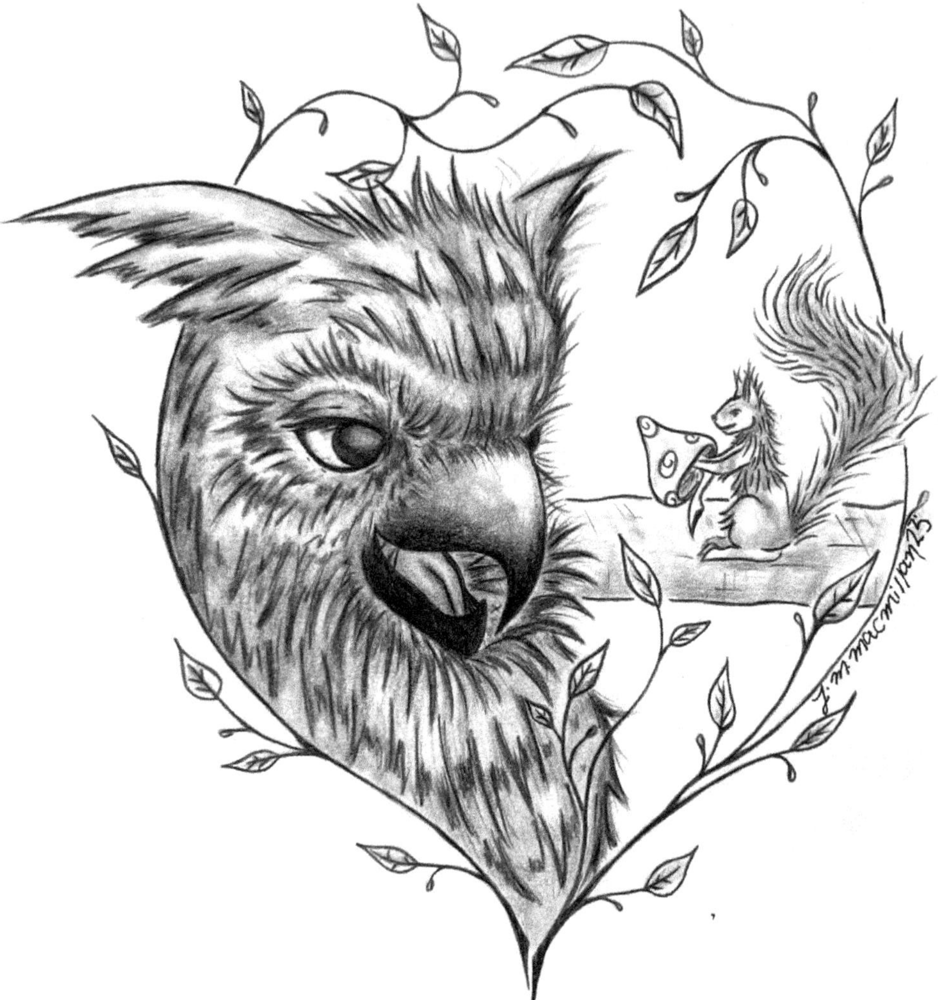
J.m.macmillan23

So I did visit, almost daily during the winter months, for there was little to do while the days were short and it was cold. We spoke of many things and I told him all I remembered of my days with my Tall and Goodboy, and in return Mervath told many tales of nature, the trees, the past and future, tales of the seven sister hawks, the hawks of old, and the wolves. He told me horrors of the wolves, but also how they raised their young and were strong, proud, and resourceful. Often I left our talks with more questions which I pondered most nights.

Winter was long and cold, the storms were few but memorable, days and nights when we would use our own warmth to warm others. The days when the sun would grace us were wonderful, especially for those who would play. Estel would not, but watch over the young that did, ever attentive of the sky. Chire and I would play but she would also play with the other young and teach them the ways of the Longtail as well. They held fear for me so I would stay away as they played and learned. There was much to keep me busy between my visits to Mervath and speaking with Estel, learning what responsibilities he held as the son of Eberges. As spring approached the world came to life and everyone rejoiced and began their spring rituals. The first leaves came and flowers thereafter. Vasetha had thawed on the West Shore and it was safe to walk about the ground during the days in Heyhin Berum. Green was the color of the Valley Of The Lion and many bird friends returned from travels south where there was no winter. Spring turned to busy summer where all helped collect what they could. The Tall came to the paths, some with beast a thread, some with snacks and wondrous foods and treats, and did I mention the snacks!

I would often follow Chire and help gather what she would gather on the West Shores, ever so often I would gaze at the East Cliffs where the Ilu flower grew. Foolish as I was, I thought I could cross the Man's Bridge and sneak up the face of the wall, bring a flower for Chire and no one would notice. We were told to stay on the West Shore as the hawks hunted the East Cliffs during the day and wolves hunted there at night. Decided I did that the next morning I would go forth with my small quest, my stealth and speed would be all I needed, and possibly return a hero of sorts. Collecting food for winter was fine and well but I think we all know my heart yearned for more. I had absorbed all the knowledge I thought important and my body was fully grown now, but I would soon find out this choice was not wise.

The morning to come did not bring the sun, for it hid in the clouds of a light rain, still many were busy gathering food for today and food still for the winter to come. Chire said her goodbyes in the morning and was off to run the errands set out for the day, and so too I was off quickly from Heyhin Berum over the fallen trees to the West Shore. It seemed very quiet, not as many Tall visit the valley on rainy days of spring, birds sung less songs and stayed in their trees. I passed over the small Man's Bridge unseen. From bush to bush, then tree to tree, I was swift and quiet, ever so often pausing to listen and look for danger. I reached the trees at the base of the East Cliff, the climb would be daunting, for I did not know a path. The ground was loose and could give way, each step was unsure and climbing the trees on the ascension could be dangerous if they gave way. Stealth and silence were my friends so up I went cautiously, over rock and fallen tree. Then ahead in the distance I saw it, the Ilu flower, it was the most wondrous thing in the valley. Five petals of white, the shape of tears, each gently overlapping the next with a sweet touch. Much of the flower's center was a soft yellow fading into the white of the petal. The very middle was small and red like that of the last sunlight, the red grew slightly into the yellow like roots of fire. In a small green bush of vines it grew up the slope, without thought I froze in awe of the Ilu. Then from behind I heard a sound! I turned and following me not far back was Chire, I stiffened.

'What are you doing, Nameless!? Have you no sense? Have you not listened to the words I speak!?' She yelled.

'Shhhh!' I tried to quiet her as I rushed down to her side.

'Do not shhh me, you have already placed us both in unnecessary danger! What are you thinking? That thou are Isper? Stop this foolishness and return at once! My father nor Estel need not hear of this.'

I did not want to say why I had come to the East Cliff but I would not lie. I prepared to explain when a gust of wind and a fierce hawk dove down upon us, we both shrieked and jumped low to the ground, then we ran. I could hear the hawk curse that its attack had failed but it turned quickly in pursuit. This was the first hawk I had seen up close, its wings were wide as the sky with claws and a beak sharp enough to slice branches. I lost sight of Chire as I tried to locate our hunter, I stumbled to a tree that led out from the cliff over the river

Vasetha. Then suddenly the hawk was upon me, just out of her grasp I ran along the tree. I knew I was being pursued. I could hear the hiss of the hawk.

'Did you think you traveled here unseen? There is no escape young Longtail, you have ventured into the lands of the sisters and will make a fine meal for my young. I am Yanom. Today I watch over the East Cliffs.'

The hawk had almost closed the distance between us when, from an unseen angle, Chire jumped on the hawks back and they smashed into a branch. The branch, Yanom and Chire fell before my eyes, I felt a great pain of helplessness. Into the rapids of Vasetha they were absorbed. I ran and jumped faster than I thought I could, jumped further than ever before but by the time I made it down to the river there was no sight of anyone. The river was fast and harsh from the rains, with the speed of a storm, and it was very deep. I was lost for what to do and felt very small in a large world with no warmth in the cold rain. I looked to the sky, above the three ravens circled.

KARTIK & TEJUIN

No time was there for wrong decisions, I had already made enough of those today. I ran down the rivers edge, my legs burned, never had I run so hard. Past Three Rock and down the East Shore of Vasetha, never did a Longtail venture this far south, it was the changing land of the Tall with many beasts, some wild. No matter how fast I could run and jump Vasetha was beyond my speed, the rains continued and slowed my pace of foot. At times I could barely see as I searched the shore but continue I must, for no forgiveness would I give myself if Chire was not found. I heard a whisper and saw a shadow and thought the hawk had returned, up I glanced and there was Mervath gliding along with me. I slowed my pace but would not stop, briefly

I explained of Chire's fall from the tree with the hawk and of my search down the river.

'Quickly I shall find Estel and call for aid, but at once I shall return to you.'

Mervath headed back to Heyhin Berum and I continued south, still unsure of all. Then luck of all luck befell me and there on the shore was the branch that fell with Chire and beyond that she lay on her back. I rushed to her side and called to her but wake she would not, though warmth was still within her. I dragged her to the shore away from Vasetha's rage, there were no trees or shelter from the rain along the eastern shore this far south. Chire still would not wake, and the light of day was fading.

'Please wake Chire, I'm so sorry, so sorry, I just wanted to bring you an Ilu flower, I'm so sorry, please wake, please wake!'

'What have we here, Tejuin' whispered a foul voice.

'Looks like a snack Kartik, no! Two snacks. Many a day since I had Longtail.' The beasts looked at me with malice and hate, they were bigger than Goodboy, the first of wolves I would see.

'Please, my friend fell in the river, will you not help us?'

'Help you!!!' Kartik laughed 'You have entered our land at a time where the sun does not show its face. We rule this land and do as we please, hunt as we please and eat as we please! Though you are but a snack and we do not usually hunt fast Longtail up trees, you would make a meal for our young brothers of the den. There is no escape for your friend who does not wake, will you share her fate or flee? Foolish Longtail.'

Frozen in fear I did not respond, though I would not run and abandon Chire. Slow and low the two wolves approached, all I could do was protect Chire as long as I could. Kartik's eyes widened and he pounced. In that instant Mervath swooped down unseen and unheard with claws splayed towards Kartik's face! A yelp went through the air, Kartik fell back but instantly regained his feet, a long scratch bled down the right side of his face, he growled and stepped back as Tejuin stepped forward towards Mervath.

'Halt you foul beast! Friends of Mervath these are!!' Mervath spread his wings full, even from behind he was magnificent.

'Old flying fool, do not stand between us and our hunt, these are our lands at night and you hold no domain here.' Tejuin slithered near as if he held no fear of Mervath's claws.

'Young wolf pup you still are in my eye, do not speak to this old owl of the laws of the Valley Of The Lion that I helped install. Yes these are your lands and you have the right to hunt all the lands here. Inturn I have the right to defend my friends to the death!' Both wolves seemed to pause at this threat. 'Or fly from fools!'

Mervath turned and grabbed Chire and I in each of his strong claws and with a flap of wing we were off away from the teeth of the wolves.

It was mystical to fly above the trees and river back to Mervath's Ledge, and on the way Chire awoke. I was relieved beyond compare but she was still weary when we landed. It seemed the rains had ceased and Estel, among others, waited for us as we arrived. It was Mervath's command for Estel to bring food and cloths to assist his sister, as if Mervath held no doubt of our return. Estel carried Chire away and she was finally safe. I was exhausted, so I sat and told Mervath of all that had transpired, with the flower, the hawk and the fall, and how it was all my fault.

'My dear Nameless, fault you will see in your own eyes, do not hold a grudge, for days are not perfect, mistakes of the young are there to learn that which the wise cannot teach. Many mistake did I make before wise I was called, this be but your first, and Chire will recover when dry, warm and rested. But I say this…..next time ask me, Mervath, and I will bring you an Ilu flower.'

Then his serious face lightened and he laughed.

Return to Heyhin Berum I did with as much haste as my legs would allow, for Chire's well being was first in thought. Second was rest.

I found Estel, he told me how Chire was well, warm and dry, and that she would stay with Masai for the night, so I slept alone that night. In that time I thought of my mistake venturing to the East Shore and though I did not ask Chire to follow I should have known that my well being was her responsibility. So even though good intentions I did have, reckless it was not to listen to the rules of the land to which I was new. Finally I did get rest, early did I wake and went to see if Chire was awake. Eberges met me first.

'Greetings Nameless, busy you have been of late, I have spoken with Mervath and all has been revealed of your venture to the East Shore. Foolish this errand was but not a waste, for much you will have learned of the Valley Of The Lion, and of your bravery in the eyes of Kartik and Tejuin. I know of these two, they are fierce and have no mercy. Lucky we are to have you and Chire safely back, I trust you will want to see her. She has begun to stir, come say your piece but quickly for she still requires rest, the struggle with Vasetha will leave her weak for some days. Afterwards come to the council platform if you would please, Masai wishes to speak to you.'

'Yes Eberges, as always your words put my mind at ease, I will come to the council without delay once I have spoken with Chire.' Slowly I entered the nest where Chire lay half awake.

'Nameless!' She said, her voice quiet and softly broken. 'So good to see you, Estel said you were unharmed but I still wanted to see for myself. He told me of the wolves and how Mervath saved us from danger.'

'You saved me first Chire, from the sister hawk. The fault of events lies with me.'

'Don't be silly Nameless, my actions have no consequence for you, I chose to jump at the hawk and you saved me from the river and the wolves. It was a fools errand to attempt to get an Ilu flower, it would have been a sweet gesture but there was no need to risk it, my heart is with yours.'

'Risk it, I did, and failed alone, much I have learned, wiser I am for my mistake. Before any other quest I will take council, only then will I decide if it is worth it to risk it.'

'Haha' Chire laughed hard. 'Risk'it! I like it! It suits you!'

I thought for a moment then laughed too.

'I love it! I have found my name!! Thank you Chire, this is the greatest gift I have ever received!' I hugged her close, then stood. 'I have been called to the council, but I shall return to check on you and bring you a snack.'

'Go then Namele…, I mean Risk'it. I will rest and await your return.'

Many were gathered, maybe all the Longtail in the valley, and Mervath sat behind the council sleeping, for long was his night, deserving of a hero's rest for the day. All were silent as I approached and sat at the center of the platform. I saw Mervath's one eye peak open and close again. To my surprise Masai rose and walked slowly before me.

'Greetings young Nameless, all have spoken of the trouble you have brought upon yourself and to my daughter Chire. All have also spoken of the one who stood between my daughter and the wolves. Many Longtail would run at the sight of the wolves, let alone look into their eyes and stand strong. As predicted by your Tall, you would find your strength.'

'Yes Masai, and I have also found my name, I will be known as Risk'it.' I said proudly.

'So let this be the end of Nameless, go forth as Risk'it and let this name bear great feats worthy of song and story.' Masai's words were strong and filled me with pride.

'Thank you all, and thank you Mervath! The listener as he sleeps, the true hero of Heyhin Berum! For he fought the wolves and saved Chire and I.'

A cheer went up from the crowd. Still Mervath slept for he cared not for praise. With that the crowd dispersed, Masai smiled at me and the council meeting was over. I raced back to Chire, she slept, warm under many cloths. There I would spend my hours tending to Chire's needs until she was better. It was but a few days til Chire was mended and we were back playing in the warmth of the sun.

It would seem my last adventures as Nameless had passed, I would go forth as Risk'it, the knowledge seeker. In the days to come busy were the Longtail, the bounty of summer had arrived, the valley flourished and bloomed. Much time did I spend in the harvest, collecting and basking in the glory of the sun. Many visitors came to the valley; migrant birds and all sorts of scavengers, the Tall would come with their beasts a string. I would watch for Goodboy and my Tall, if they should visit the Valley, but they did not. I spoke with many Tall that would visit, often like the tales told they would bring great wondrous snacks from afar. I would always bring what I had received to share with Chire as she was busy most days with the new young of the spring, teaching was her way, and her heart. I would not ask her to come with me, but to remain and await my return. Many days I spoke with Mervath of what I would have to do if I wanted to find my mother and my kin in the lands of the stone nests of the Tall. Perilous it would be, resources unknown, safety from storms may not exist, the many beasts of the Tall, and the hawks that venture far from nest to hunt in the lands of less trees. On the eve of my leaving I explained to Chire best I could; 'If I had lost my young I would want to know if they survived and were grown, for losing a child must be the greatest fear of any parent.' She understood, as most would, so I set forth with guidance from the Longtail of the Valley of the Lion and Mervath's wise words. 'Grave perils lay before your quest, Risk'it, the knowledge seeker, what you will find is your destiny, do not stray from the path of heart, look for friends in scary places and fear not, for in your great need Mervath may appear but take it upon thyself to save the day, for days will come when others will need you to be their hero. May your wisdom guide you to bravery when most would run.'

'Thank you Mervath, for all. Deeds cannot be repaid, but let friendship live eternal.'

'Oh and don't forget to return to us young Risk'it, for I will wish to hear all tales. A great feast will be had and we shall sleep safely and smile under the sun.'

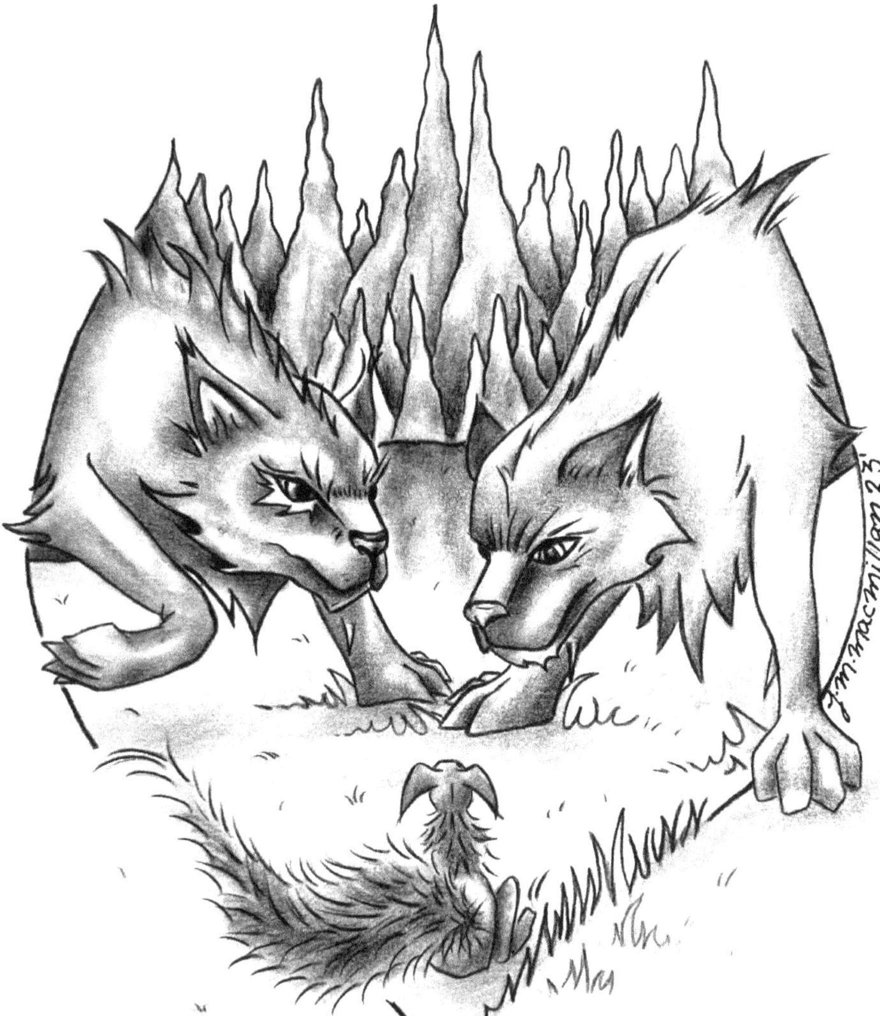
J.M.MacMillan 23'

GOODBOY

The Realm Of Archirm

Dark is the night that I watch, evils worthy of fear grow and multiply there. Though I am dark as the night, do not fear me, for I am as my Master, protector of the small. Only evil need fear me and my tooth and claw, for I see and hear all in the night, and that which I do not see or hear, I smell before it enters my realm. Seem it might that I be asleep at my post, but at a moments notice I am ready to heed the call of my Master. My Master requires rest from the day, so at night I watch and protect those who would protect me. Rise with the sun my Master will, to the yard of back he will take me. I will inspect my grandfather's land, for many friends stir and play in the night. As my Master readies himself for the deeds of the day I too prepare, for most days are full of adventure. Keep watch of my lands I do, from path to park, greetings received by many who dwell in my realm. Praised I am, but not for my strength, size or bark! But for the peace we keep in my land, for peace is the quest of all heroes. The strong must protect the small.

Far we travel to see friends of old, always in search of friends of new. Collecting supplies with my Master, together we will feast when the day is done. Always together, safe in our pack though it may be small, one mustn't underestimate its strength. Many tree and bush we keep watch, from valley to forest, always watching for the safety of the small. After such days one must rest and eat hearty, for one never knows what perils the future will hold. HARK!! The horn of Doorfront Pass! Like lightning I move, like thunder my bark! All in my realm know my bark and those who visit will learn to respect it. But all is well, a bringer of letters who comes on the daily was at the door. Forever vigilant I stay, for like my Master I protect that which is most precious. Among other things my master creates great feasts and he rests, for days are long though years go fast. Night approaches, ready my watch I will, for the night is dark in my realm but fear not, for it is I who keep watch.

Milton Keynes UK
Ingram Content Group UK Ltd.
UKHW012146161123
432728UK00002B/19